characters created by
lauren child

I am EXTREMELY
absolutely
boiling

PUFFIN

Text based on the script written by Bridget Hurst

Illustrations from the TV animation produced by Tiger Aspe

PUFFIN BOOKS
Published by the Penguin Group: London, New York, Australia,
Canada, India, Ireland, New Zealand and South Africa
Penguin Books Ltd, Registered Offices: 80 Strand, London WC2R 0RL, England

puffinbooks.com

This edition published in Great Britain in Puffin Books 2012
001 – 10 9 8 7 6 5 4 3 2 1
Text and illustrations copyright © Lauren Child/Tiger Aspect Productions Limited, 2008
Charlie and Lola word and logo ® and © Lauren Child, 2005
Charlie and Lola is produced by Tiger Aspect Productions
All rights reserved
The moral right of the author/illustrator has been asserted
Manufactured in China
ISBN: 978-0-718-19527-4
This edition produced for the Book People Ltd,
Hall Wood Avenue, Haydock, St Helens, WA11 9UL

I have this little sister Lola.
She is small and very funny.
"I am also extremely absolutely BOILING!
And the only thing that will make me
completely NOT boiling any more
is a strawberry ice cream!"

Outside in the shade,
I ask, "Arnold, why are you panting?"

Arnold says,
"Dogs keep cool by panting.
I'm trying to see if it works."

Lola says,
"Could you pant more quieter please?"

Then I say,
"I hear the ice-cream truck!"

Lola says, "Yum, strawberry!"

"Mmm... yummy," says Arnold.

Then Lola says, "I know, Arnold!
I'll taste your ice cream and
then you can taste mine."

"OK. Me first," says Arnold.

Arnold takes a big lick of
Lola's ice cream, but when
Lola tries to take it back...

"Oh no!" shouts Lola. "My ice cream is COMPLETELY all over the floor!"

"Maybe Arnold will **share** his ice cream with you," I say.

So Lola asks, "Arnold, will you share your ice cream with me?"

But Arnold says, "No."

And Lola says, "You are not my **favourite** or my **best**. I will not ever **never** forgive you!"

Later, Lola says,
    "Ice is good for **cooling**,
but not as nice-tasting as ice cream."

"I wish we were in
        the North Pole," I say.

"Yes," Lola says.
"Where it is completely
freezing cold."

Marv and Morton pass by
    on their way to the swimming pool.

Lola asks,
    "Can we come, too?"

But Marv says,
        "Sorry, Lola. There isn't any room in
the car. Maybe you could play with Arnold?"

"I'm not playing with him,"
        says Lola. "He's a **Meanie!**"

Instead of going to the pool,
Lola and I make a waterfall.

"All the water's gone,"
Lola says.

"That's OK," I say.
            "We'll get more from the hose."

That's when we see Arnold...
and his pool.

So I say,
    "That would DEFINITELY cool us down.
Don't you think, Lola?"

    But Lola says,
        "Come on, Charlie..."

"It might be a really, really good idea to
forgive Arnold," I say. "Then maybe
you can play in a real pool."

"But he didn't share OR say he's sorry,"
says Lola.

"Well, he looks sorry," I say.

"Does he?" Lola asks.

Then Arnold calls out,
"Lola, would you like to sit in my pool?"

Lola finally says, "Yes, please."

And Arnold says,
    "I'm sorry about the ice cream, Lola."

"That's OK," says Lola.
    "Do you want to play squirty bottles?"

"Yes, please," he says.

"Charlie!" Lola shouts. "Can you pass
                 Arnold a squirty bottle?"

"I can't," I say. "Arnold's dad gave us ice lollies!"

"ICE LOLLIES!" Lola says.

PLOP!
Arnold's ice lolly falls into the pool.

"My ice lolly!" says Arnold.

So Lola asks,
"Do you want a bit of mine?"

And Arnold says, "Thanks, Lola."

But then...

PLOP!

Lola's ice lolly falls into the pool, too.

"Oops," Arnold says.

And Lola says, "Charlie...?"